THE
ALL-SEEING
BOY
AND THE
BLUE SKY OF
HAPPINESS

THE
ALL-SEEING
BOY
AND THE
BLUE SKY OF
HAPPINESS

A CHILDREN'S PARABLE
BY
NICK KETTLES

ILLUSTRATED BY SERENA SAX HALLAM

Snow Lion Publications
Ithaca, New York

Snow Lion Publications
P.O. Box 6483
Ithaca, New York 14851 USA
607-273-8519
www.snowlionpub.com

Copyright © 2011 Nicholas Andrew Kettles

ISBN 978-1-55939-371-3
ISBN 1-55939-371-8

Printed in Korea

Library of Congress Cataloging-in-Publication Data

Kettles, Nick.
  The All-Seeing Boy and the blue sky of happiness : a children's parable / by Nick
Kettles ; illustrated by Serena Sax Hallam.
      p. cm.
  Summary: The All-Seeing Boy has always yearned to take away other people's
sadness, and one day a hobo in a ruby-red coat teaches him how to find and use the
magic that he has always believed existed.
  ISBN-13: 978-1-55939-371-3 (alk. paper)
  ISBN-10: 1-55939-371-8 (alk. paper)
  [1. Contentment--Fiction. 2. Helpfulness--Fiction. 3. Conduct of life--Fiction. 4.
Magic--Fiction. 5. Parables.] I. Hallam, Serena Sax, 1969- ill. II. Title.
  PZ7.K4946All 2011
  [Fic]--dc22
                          2010042307

892890

To Cairo, on your ninth birthday.
Your happiness is a gift to the world.

The All-Seeing Boy lived an ordinary life—
each day getting up, washed, and dressed,
then going to school to listen, learn, and
play, before coming home to eat, play some more, and go
to bed. He was mostly happy, especially when the people
around him—the people he loved—were also happy. But
when the people that he loved were not so happy, perhaps
a little sad, he would wonder what it was that he could do
to help them. It was at times like these that he wished with
all his heart that there was something—some power, some
magic, something really big—that he could call upon to
help lift their troubles away. And the more he thought about
helping those who were sad or down, the more he sensed
that something really *was* within his grasp.

He sensed it sparkling in the air, on days when the rain
had just passed; he imagined that he could hear it in the still
of the early morning when there was seemingly nothing to
hear; could almost smell it at the sunset just before the sun
dipped below the skyline and melted into inky blackness.

What was it? How would it help? Could anyone find it?

He tried to tell his friends at school, but they didn't seem to understand. They called him day-dreamer, and weird. Not liking this, the All-Seeing Boy learned not to share his sense of wonder about the hidden world of magic he sometimes felt. But still he yearned to know what it was.

Then, one day, an answer came quite suddenly.

At the end of the street of terraced houses in which the All-Seeing Boy lived, there was a thrift store. Inside, it was piled high with black plastic draw-string garbage bags overflowing with donated, musty second-hand clothes waiting to be hung on rusty silver chrome rails.

He had often seen a large, elderly lady inside, working feverishly to make everything tidy, although he suspected she never would.

Outside this thrift store sat a hobo. He was there each day the All-Seeing Boy went to school, and each day when he returned home—collecting pennies in a paper cup, nodding in thanks to those passers-by who didn't just pass by.

The lines on the hobo's weathered face were deep with dirt and grime, and his greasy white hair was mostly hidden under a flat cap pulled down over his eyes. He wore old black leather shoes, with soles that peeled away from the toe, and strangely, a long red woolen winter coat. Its color was the deepest, most intense ruby red the All-Seeing Boy had ever seen.

Other hobos he had seen were mostly dressed in dull colors—tired blacks, browns, beiges, and grays—that faded into the background of blacks, browns, beiges, and grays of city life. But, with a coat of deepest red like this one, it was difficult to miss him. There was something just so wonderful about his ruby-red overcoat that brightened up the street. He was part of the scenery, and in fact had been around the All-Seeing Boy's street for longer than any of the residents could remember. Some even joked whether it was the ruby-coated hobo who kept an eye on the thrift store, or the thrift store lady who kept an eye on the ruby-coated hobo. Either way, it didn't matter. They liked to have him around.

The All-Seeing Boy liked him too, and, acting on his mother's encouragement to help others, would always walk home on the hobo's side of the street to place a few pennies into his cup. Every day, the ruby-coated hobo with his cap pulled down over his eyes would nod his head in silent thanks.

And so it continued, until one very fine day, when the skies were especially blue, the ruby-coated hobo looked up and smiled the widest smile the All-Seeing Boy had ever seen. The All-Seeing Boy froze as for the first time he took in the hobo's bright blue eyes. They were so soft and warm that the All-Seeing Boy was quite astounded. He had seen hobos' eyes before, but they had always been dull with sadness, just like the clothes they wore. But the ruby-coated hobo's eyes were alive. His smile, too, revealed a set of perfect, pearly white teeth, with one beautiful glinting gold tooth on the top row. The All-Seeing Boy was really surprised by the hobo's face, which showed a person not at all like what he had expected. Perhaps it was the gold tooth. Suddenly he thought that maybe the hobo had once been a rich man, a really rich man.

"Yes I was," replied the ruby-coated hobo joyfully.

The All-Seeing Boy was startled. "How did you know, I mean, I didn't say anything," stammered the All-Seeing Boy.

"How did I know what you were thinking?"

"Yes, that's it, *how* did you know?"

"I know because I heard your thought whispering in the wind, when you stopped to look at me."

"Wow!" exclaimed the All-Seeing Boy. "How did you learn to do that?"

"Just by sitting here, watching life," replied the ruby-coated hobo.

"But that's silly. How does watching life teach you to hear what other people are thinking?"

"Sitting still and watching life can teach you many things, my boy."

The All-Seeing Boy hesitated for a moment, before the ruby-coated hobo held out his hand and introduced himself. "Mr. Jason Carper Esquire, at your service."

The All-Seeing Boy took Jason Carper's hand, and as he did so, he felt a tingle of electricity that made his hair bristle. What a very strange name, he thought to himself. Very strange. Jason Carper. Esquire.

He felt just a little nervous, but then he noticed how soft and gentle the hobo's hand was, and suddenly relaxing, felt a surge of wonder fill his mind. Maybe, just maybe, the hobo with the ruby-red coat could answer his question. And before he knew it, he had blurted it out. "There's something big in life, isn't there, something more than what we see?"

Jason Carper grinned a little and nodded.

"Want to know what it is?"

The All-Seeing Boy nodded eagerly. Jason Carper took a deep breath and looked deep into the All-Seeing Boy's eyes for what seemed an eternity, before he spoke.

Then he began.

"When I was a rich man, I worked for a very successful company in the City of London. I wore a smart, very expensive suit to work. And on cold mornings I would walk proudly down the street wearing this ruby-red coat, enjoying how it drew attention to me. I had my name, Jason

Carper, Esq., embossed in gold letters on the door of my office, at the top of a very tall building. I worked hard, and was very, very busy. I was a very important man. Many people worked for me. I knew their names, but only to tell them what to do, to help the company to make more money. I never took the time to really know the people I worked with, to know if they were happy or sad. I never had time to think about anyone other than myself. When I walked to work I would be thinking about all the money I would make that day for myself. When I ate my lunch I was thinking about all the money I would make after lunch, and when I went to bed, the money I would make the next day. So, as you can see, I spent a lot of time thinking about myself."

"Is it bad to only think about yourself?" interrupted the All-Seeing Boy.

"Not particularly," replied Jason Carper, "but it can make you very lonely."

"But how could you have been lonely if you were so successful? You could have had anything you wanted!"

"That's true," sighed Jason Carper. "And I did. But nothing lasts forever. As you can see, I am no longer a young man!"

The All-Seeing Boy laughed. It was true, everybody changes.

Jason Carper continued his story.

"Then, one day, the company closed, almost overnight, without warning—the owner had not paid his taxes, they said—and I had no job. I became very sad. Very quickly. All the things I had bought didn't mean much after I wasn't so important anymore."

"What did you do?" asked the All-Seeing Boy eagerly.

The ruby-coated hobo laughed. "I didn't know what to do! All I had ever known was how to work for the company where I had worked since I left school. So I just sat watching TV, until I had no money left. Then, the bank that owned my apartment said I had to leave. I left with just my shoes, suit, a cap, and a little money in the pocket of my thick woolen ruby-red coat. That's when I came to live on the street. I lived for many years on the street still feeling very sorry for myself. Very sad. I would always think to myself, what use am I to the world? I used to be so important, but what use am I now?"

"So even when you were poor, you were still thinking about yourself," said the All-Seeing Boy.

In his excitement, his anticipation, the All-Seeing Boy hadn't realized that they were now walking together, up the street towards the park. The ruby-coated hobo was much taller than he had expected, taking long, loping strides, seemingly floating along. The All-Seeing Boy felt like he was floating along, too.

Jason Carper turned to him, smiled, and nodded his head. "That's right. I just sat on the street, feeling sorry for myself, watching people walking to and fro for a long time. But then I noticed something interesting."

"What was that?"

"I noticed that every time the sun came out people would smile, but when there were grey clouds, which was most of the time, they frowned and looked sad."

"That's not interesting, that's just what people do," said the All-Seeing Boy, interrupting.

"Ah, but why do people do this? That's what I wanted to know. Why was it that people were like the weather, like the sky—happy for just a moment, when the sun comes out revealing the turquoise blue sky, then sad when the grey clouds cover its warmth."

"How long did it take you to find an answer?" quizzed the All-Seeing Boy.

"Oh, about a year or two," giggled Jason Carper. "Not long for someone who has time on their hands. But I can tell you that when I finally realized why people were like the weather, I wasn't sad anymore. In fact it made me so happy I laughed out loud."

"Why did you laugh?" asked the All-Seeing Boy, a little confused.

"I laughed because I realized the sky is always blue."

"Is that all? Why is that funny?" inquired the All-Seeing Boy, secretly hoping this wasn't the only answer to his question.

"It's funny because it's so simple," said Jason Carper quietly. "People think they have no control over whether they are happy or sad, but the grey clouds of their sadness are just like curtains covering a window. Just because the window can't be seen doesn't mean it's not there. Happiness is like the blue sky, it is always there, it never goes away, it just gets hidden by grey sad clouds. People forget it's there because they choose to watch the clouds instead."

"So people aren't really sad," added the All-Seeing Boy.

"That's right!" exclaimed Jason Carper, joyfully. "They just think they are!"

"They've forgotten the blue sky," laughed the All-Seeing Boy, running alongside excitedly.

"Yes, they have forgotten the blue sky of happiness."

The ruby-coated hobo and the All-Seeing Boy laughed together for a very long time, before the All-Seeing Boy noticed everything was silent and they were now on top of the hill at the center of the park and could see the city far below. The sky was indeed blue and the golden yolk sun was low in the sky, yet still warm to the skin.

"Is the blue sky of happiness the something big I can feel sometimes?" asked the All-Seeing Boy.

"No, the something big you can feel is more than the blue sky of happiness."

"What is it, I want to know. I know there is magic in this life. What is it?" pressed the All-Seeing Boy eagerly.

Jason Carper looked at the All-Seeing Boy intensely, then replied: "*The magic you can sense is what you will feel when you remember the blue sky of happiness for other people.*"

The All-Seeing Boy opened his eyes wide with astonishment: "Is that why thinking only about yourself can be so lonely?"

Jason Carper nodded sagely in reply.

The All-Seeing Boy felt a surge of excitement: "How do I remember the blue sky of happiness for other people—I can't make their clouds of sadness disappear for them, can I?"

Jason Carper leaned on the back of a bench and let out a gentle sigh. "Oh, you can do many things for other people," he said. "How you think about other people affects what they feel. If you see them as sad, then that's how they will be, but if you see them as happy…"

"Even when they're sad?" interrupted the All-Seeing Boy.

"Exactly," said Jason Carper. "Then you help to dissolve the grey clouds for them."

"But how do I see them happy?" asked the All-Seeing Boy.

Jason Carper laughed gently, then replied: "You imagine what they would be doing if they didn't have a care in the world, and the sun was shining, and the sky was blue, free from clouds."

"Is that it?" asked the All-Seeing Boy in amazement.

"Yep. Want to try?" offered Jason Carper.

The All-Seeing Boy eagerly replied that he would.

The ruby-coated hobo scanned the field below them. After a short while, he pointed to a man walking his dog some way down the path. The man didn't look happy. He had his collar turned up; his face, etched with worry lines, was fixed firmly on the path at his feet; and he kept impatiently pulling his dog, who wanted to sniff at anything and everything.

"He will do," said Jason Carper.

"Why him?" said the All-Seeing Boy.

Jason Carper looked sombre as he said, "Because today, as you can see, the sky is already blue, and still he doesn't notice. It is people like him who need the help of blue-sky thoughts the most."

When the All-Seeing Boy heard this, he felt the magic within his grasp. He knew that he wanted to help this man to remember the blue sky of happiness. He didn't know why he wanted to help this man, whom he had never met before, but he felt it deep within his heart. It was just like the longing he had felt for so long to know the answer to his big question, that there must be something more to life.

"So!" said Jason Carper more upbeat. "What would this man be doing if he knew the sun was shining and the sky was blue and free from clouds?"

The All-Seeing Boy closed his eyes and thought for a while. Then opening them, he smiled and said, "He would be running and laughing, playing gently with his dog, and then, once they had run as much as they could, he would be lying on the grass, smiling at the sunset."

"That's lovely," said Jason Carper.

"But how will he hear my blue sky thoughts?"

"Just like the way a TV receives its programs. You send blue sky thoughts like pictures floating on a wave, rippling through the air."

"Wow, b-b-but, how will he *hear* them? I mean I can only hear the thoughts inside my own head, and you said it took a long time watching life before you could hear other people's thoughts."

"That's right. It does take a long time to recognize whose thoughts you're listening to. To tell the difference between your own and those of others. But blue-sky thoughts, when they are sent with love,"—the All-Seeing Boy's eyes opened even wider— "just slip right in, between all their grey-cloud sad thoughts, and… well, they just assume it was their own."

"Just like that?" asked the All-Seeing Boy.

"Yep, just like that."

"Amazing!" exclaimed the All-Seeing Boy.

"Want to know how to send them?" offered Jason Carper.

The All-Seeing Boy nodded.

"First, you have to close your eyes…" The boy did so and then listened to the instructions of Mr. Jason Carper, Esq., the ruby-coated hobo, as he described in a very soft voice how to send blue sky of happiness thoughts to people who couldn't imagine there was anything better to think about than their own sad grey-cloud thoughts.

"In your imagination," he began, "first picture the blue sky free from clouds. Let the blue in your blue sky be so bright it almost sparkles. So bright, so clear, that it brings a smile to your face. Then, imagine that the blue sky is sinking into you. Down, through the top of your head, through your body, into your heart and every cell of your body. Feel the blue sky fill your very being with happiness, so you can imagine it for others with greater feeling.

Now, picture the man doing what he would be doing if he knew that the sky was always blue—playing and running happily with his dog, feeling the warm breeze in his hair, smelling the sweet grass beneath his feet. Then, later, feeling his heartbeat as he lies on his back, smiling, with his dog beside him, gazing at the golden sun as it sets below the horizon, until the blue sky is aflame with its regal light. Really feel this image, and then imagine it riding on a golden wave through the air, traveling from your heart, to his. *Softly through the air like a feather in the breeze.* And when it reaches him, his heart, it dissolves into a haze of warm golden light that expands to surround him from head to toe."

Jason Carper's voice trailed away, and when the All-Seeing Boy noticed that he had stopped talking, he became aware of a warm glow inside *his* heart.

He opened his eyes and, to his disappointment, noticed that Jason Carper, the ruby-coated hobo, had gone. The All-Seeing Boy quickly scanned the horizon but he was nowhere to be seen. The park was empty except for a man running joyfully with his dog. The All-Seeing Boy watched the man with his dog for some time before he realized that it was the same man to whom he had sent his blue-sky thoughts. The man's grey clouds of sadness had lifted!

The All-Seeing Boy watched the man reach the gate at the end of the park, and then began walking back towards his home. As he did so, he felt a wonderful fizzing feeling in his legs that tingled nicely, moving up his body, just like getting into a warm bath. He looked around and everything seemed just right, just so. Nothing right, nothing wrong, just so. It was a magical feeling. It was *the* magic, that he had always felt was there, somewhere outside of himself, but now he knew that it was inside him. And what's more he knew how to find it.

That night the All-Seeing Boy dreamed of Mr. Jason Carper Esquire riding a wonderful white snow-lion through emerald-green, grassy plains below sparkling, snow-capped mountains. His ruby-red hobo's coat was now a ruby-red robe down to his ankles with gold bands around the sleeves. His greasy hair was now short, white and fluffy. His glowing, golden, moonlike face was free of lines, and his blue sapphire eyes were shining. As he watched Jason Carper ride his white snow-lion, he heard him say: *My boy! There are many worlds to be journeyed, many gifts to be discovered. The key to both can be found in the blue sky of happiness.*

Jason Carper rode his white snow-lion off into the distance, with his ruby-red robe flowing behind him, until suddenly a rainbow bridge appeared between two mountains, and Jason Carper disappeared in a flash of light.

The All-Seeing Boy awoke with a start. It was Saturday. The thrift store. He must get there to see Jason Carper. With urgency he jumped out of bed, dressed hurriedly, and dashed out. He ran down to the bottom of the road in which he lived, his heart thumping. But when the All-Seeing Boy arrived, Jason Carper was not there. His usual space, the same space that he had occupied for longer than the All-Seeing Boy could remember, was empty.

The All-Seeing Boy looked around, up the street and back. But he was nowhere to be seen. He turned to look inside the thrift store. There inside was the same large, elderly woman, as always sorting out piles upon piles of musty clothes. She looked up at him and frowned. The All-Seeing Boy could feel she didn't want him leaning up against the shop window, and normally he would have simply walked away, but just as he was about to do so, she pulled out a bright ruby-red coat from yet another black plastic drawstring garbage bag, and proceeded to place it on a hanger, and then on a rusty chrome rail.

The All-Seeing Boy's heart leapt, and before he knew it, he had entered the shop.

"Can I help you," barked the old lady grumpily.

"I'm looking for a coat," said the All-Seeing Boy.

"They're all on the rail here, fitting room at the back," replied the old lady.

The All-Seeing Boy tried not to look too excited as he made straight for the ruby-red coat. He took it from its hanger and walked over to the fitting room. It was the same coat. It just had to be. He put it on, and admired himself in the mirror. It was a little long, but it was quite warm, and clean, too.

He thrust his hands into the pockets, wrapping it closer around his front. As he did so, deep inside one of the pockets, he felt a small piece of paper. He pulled it out. It was a business card. Written across the front in gold-embossed letters were the words "Jason Carper, Esq." and below that, the words "*Blue Sky Thinking.*"

The All-Seeing Boy stopped for a moment, remembering his wonderful walk with Jason Carper, and how he had learned to help people remember the blue sky of happiness. He looked at himself again in the mirror, and it was then that he noticed, in the distance behind his reflection, the old lady with her hand on her head. Her face was white, and she seemed to be very tired and in some pain. Behind her were the piles of clothes that she never seemed to be able to tidy.

He knew what to do. Closing his eyes he first imagined the blue sky free from clouds, so bright, so clear, sinking into him, filling every cell of his body with joy and happiness. Then he imagined the old lady in the back garden of a small terraced house, on a warm sunny day. The sky a brilliant, turquoise blue, free from clouds. The sun golden. She was tending to many beautiful sweet-scented pink geraniums in large terracotta pots. In his mind, the All-Seeing Boy imagined her bending down to smell their intoxicating perfume, while humming along to a gentle jazz song from the radio.

The All-Seeing Boy imagined his blue sky thought floating through the air on a golden wave from his heart, floating softly to the old lady's heart, where it surrounded her in a haze of golden light.

Slowly opening his eyes, the All-Seeing Boy placed Jason Carper's business card in his jeans pocket, took off the coat, replaced it on its hanger, and walked over to place it back on a rail. As he was doing so, he noticed that the old lady was now behind the counter busily tuning an old transistor radio. He paused to watch while she found the station she wanted. Gentle, big band jazz music floated out into the shop, and the old lady began to hum sweetly. She looked up and offered the All-Seeing Boy a smile. He smiled back and felt his heart warm once more, tingling with the magic.

*To find out more about The Blue Sky of Happiness meditation
please visit www.blueskyofhappiness.com*

Acknowledgments

Thank you, Josh, for your Blue Sky inspiration—you can indeed feel it sinking into you. Thanks to Serena for bringing this story so beautifully to life, and ensuring the first 1000 readers. Also to Susie Taylor, Dr. Jo Nash, Seb Leduc, web design maestro Neil Scott, Olivier @ Zookeeper, Francisco at Social Mouths, Claudia von Januszkiewicz, Charles Lewis, all the bees, and beekeepers Rick and LA, for your dedicated support in developing the vision of a more loving world when it was just an idea. To my beautiful daughters Asha and Eloa, for your constant reminder of the primary importance of fun and play in life; HH The Dalai Lama for encouraging me to put this story in service of a bigger game; to Sidney Piburn for taking a chance; Henry, Karen, and Laura for your genius and compassion; my wonderful mother for the gift of perseverance; and finally but most especially, to my beloved Priya for your steadfast support, love, and tenderness.

Tibetan Children's Village

A percentage of the author's and illustrator's proceeds from this book will go towards supporting SOS Children's Villages' work with the Tibetan community. Shortly after many Tibetans fled from their native country in the late 1950s, the Dalai Lama founded the Tibetan Children's Villages. In 1971, the first Tibetan SOS Children's Village was built in Dharamsala, a city in northern India where a large number of refugees had settled.

For over 7,000 children these SOS Villages mean a permanent home, while the various additional facilities, including schools, day-care centers, and workshops for training apprenticeships, serve the needs of a further 6,000 children and youngsters. Today, the work of SOS Children's Villages remains vital, as every year more children arrive from Tibet.

If you enjoyed reading *The All-Seeing Boy and the Blue Sky of Happiness* and are inspired by its message of loving-kindness, please also consider making a donation to The Tibetan Children's Villages by visiting: http://sos-usa.org/bluesky